Top of the Class

Adapted by Heather Alexander

Based on the series created by Todd J. Greenwald

Based on the episodes, "Wizard School Part I," Written by Vince Cheung & Ben Montanio
and "Wizard School Part II," Written by Gigi McCreery & Perry Rein

New York

visit us at www.abdopublishing.com

Reinforced library bound edition published in 2011 by Spotlight, a division of ABDO Group, 8000 West 78th Street, Edina, Minnesota 55439. This edition reprinted by arrangement with Disney Press, an imprint of Disney Book Group, LLC. www.disneybooks.com

Printed in the United States of America, Melrose Park, Illinois.
042010
092010
 This book contains at least 10% recycled materials.

Library of Congress Cataloging-in-Publication Data
This title was previously cataloged with the following information:

Alexander, Heather.
Top of the class / Adapted by Heather Alexander.
  p. cm. (Wizards of waverly place ; #5)
 I. Title. II. Series: Wizards of Waverly Place.

[Fic]--dc22   2008924989

ISBN 978-1-59961-752-7 (reinforced library edition)

All Spotlight books have reinforced library binding and are manufactured in the United States of America.

Chapter One

Alex Russo had a huge smile across her face. Today was the best day of the year. It was even better than Christmas. Even better than her birthday. Maybe even better, she thought, than Christmas and her birthday *combined*.

It was the last day of school!

Just thinking about the day made her happy. No homework, no tests, and no teachers—for two whole glorious months! Alex pushed her long, dark hair out of her eyes and darted through the crowded hallway of Tribeca Prep. Kids whooped and celebrated as they cleaned out their lockers. She waved to her best friend, Harper Evans, and then hurried over to her sixteen-year-old brother, Justin.

As Justin pulled a book from his locker, Alex peeked in and gasped. His locker was so neat, so organized, so . . . unlike her locker. She hadn't dared open her own locker in two days. There was a pretty good chance that a year's worth of forgotten homework assignments and work sheets would tumble out and bury her.

"How was your last day of school, Alex?" Justin asked.

Alex sighed. "Oh, tough. So many people were signing my yearbook, I ran out of room. I had to get a second yearbook." She glanced at the blue leather book in her hands.

"How did you get a second yearbook?"

Justin asked suspiciously. "They're all gone."
But as soon as he said it, Justin knew the
answer. He searched his locker. Just as he had
suspected, his yearbook was missing. "Where's
my yearbook, Alex?"

"Come on, Justin," Alex replied. "Hardly
anybody signed it, and one of them was you."

"Yeah. . . ." Justin stalled for time. It wasn't
easy having a sister who was one of the most
popular girls in school. "Maybe I was saving
room for friends."

"Like who?" Alex teased.

"Vice Principal Clements, Earl the crossing
guard, my biology teacher, and all the ladies in
the front office," Justin replied smugly.

Alex straightened her red flowered hoodie
and smiled knowingly. "So, basically, all your
friends are adults."

"Yeah, well, I fit in best with adults. I'm
very mature." Justin liked the sound of that.
Maybe it would remind Alex that he was two

years older than she was. Maybe she would respect him more.

Suddenly, a loud voice came through on the hallway intercom. "*Will Justin Russo report to Lost and Found? We have your cape and light-saber.*"

Several kids near them stopped talking and stared at Justin and Alex. Alex turned beet red.

"Hmm." Justin shut his locker and marched past Alex to the office to pick up his stuff. Maybe he'd get the secretaries there to sign his light-saber. *That* would show Alex.

Alex rolled her eyes. "I can't believe they found where I hid those," she muttered, heading for the main doors. It was time to leave. No more Tribeca Prep for her! Even better, no more being embarrassed by Justin in school. At least not for another two months.

Two hours later, Alex was back in class. Sure, regular school was over. But, obviously, her dad hadn't gotten the memo. He was still adamant about holding wizard classes, even though her main school year had just ended. Summer didn't seem to mean "hang out and chill" in the magical world.

Alex was a wizard. So was Justin and their twelve-year-old brother, Max. Their dad, Jerry, was also a wizard, but he had lost his powers when he married their mom, Theresa, who was a mortal. In wizard families, all the kids got their powers when they turned twelve. But the rule was that only one child in each family could keep his or her powers when they became adults. The kid who performed magic the best won the title of family wizard.

It was a little hard to keep everything straight, but not as hard for Alex as keeping her magical powers a secret. No one outside the family—not even her best friend, Harper—knew about her magical powers. And no one could know—*ever*.

Alex thought wizard class was *so* boring. She put her feet up on the round coffee table shortly after class started and let out a sigh. She was already antsy. But luckily, her dad didn't care about the feet-on-the-table stuff the way her mom did. And the Wizard's Lair, where class was always held, was Dad's territory.

The lair was what Dad called the basement of their brownstone apartment building in New York City. The family's sandwich shop, the Waverly Sub Station, was on the main floor, and the family lived on the top floors. The cluttered basement room was another huge secret. They entered through a door disguised to look like a freezer in the restaurant's kitchen. The room was filled with spell books, bottles of brightly colored potions, and a lot of other enchanted things. Here, their dad taught them magic and how to become wizards.

While magic was fun, practicing how to use it and learning how to control its powers could be hard. It wasn't all just wave the wand and—poof! Many things could go wrong, as Alex had found out time after time. Magic had to be studied and protected—and studying just wasn't Alex's thing.

Mr. Russo was still teaching when he suddenly began to wave his arms to get his children's attention. He looked like he was about to burst with anticipation.

"You know how regular wizard mail can sometimes take up to an hour?" their dad asked excitedly. "Well, now we have WIPS—Wizard Instant Parcel Service. You can send mail instantly."

"You mean like e-mail?" Alex observed, wondering if her dad could *really* be so clueless.

"No, no, no," her dad answered quickly. "Let me show you. You do it with this." Magically, a large, silver, old-fashioned key appeared in his hand.

"An old key, wow," Alex said sarcastically.

"Ooh!" Max teased, pretending to be impressed.

Mr. Russo gritted his teeth. "Okay. Make fun, but watch this. Here, Alex, take this key and go over there." Alex stood up and reached her hand out for the key. She walked behind the sofa. "Now, open a portal mail slot in midair," her father instructed.

"Really?" Alex loved when her dad allowed them to actually *do* magic. It was so much more fun than learning about spells and history from heavy, dusty books. "Okay." She held up the key and turned it.

Instantly, a gold aura appeared in the air! The circle shimmered and sparkled around where the key had been.

"If you say, '*mailus-spontaneous*' followed by a name or a place, the envelope will go there," instructed Mr. Russo. Then her father handed her a large yellow envelope. "Here, send this to Justin."

"*Mailus-spontaneous-Justin-Russo.*" Alex touched the envelope to the golden aura. The hole immediately sucked the letter out of her hand, and the whole thing disappeared!

Then, across the room, the envelope dropped out of the air and into Justin's lap. "It worked." Justin grinned. "Hey, that was fast." Suddenly, another golden aura shimmered above him, and a wooden bird with a card taped to its back plopped into his lap. Justin grabbed the bird, and his eyes lit up. "It's a messenger pigeon from Wiz Tech!" he cried. He pulled off the card from the bird's back and jumped up from his chair. "They've accepted me for summer boarding school." He waved the card victoriously.

"Well, of *course* they accepted you. Who else would want to go?" Alex chuckled. Even a bribe of twenty new pairs of shoes couldn't get her to go to school in the summer. Having to attend wizard classes was enough!

"Lots of people," Justin replied. "If you get into Wiz Tech, you're a shoo-in for Transylvania State."

Alex gasped, pretending she was impressed. "You mean it gets *better*?"

"And you know the best part about Wiz Tech?" Justin informed his dad. "I get a whole summer away from, uh, you know who." He nodded toward his sister.

"I know you mean me," Alex scoffed. "And that's totally unfair."

Suddenly, Justin let out a huge shriek. Max had suddenly dropped out of the air! He landed with a loud thud next to him. Justin just looked over at his younger brother and rolled his eyes. Max never took wizard class seriously.

"Awesome!" Max cried. He had just traveled by the magical parcel service! "Hey!" he called to Alex. "Let's scare Justin again."

Alex laughed. She and Max loved playing

jokes on Justin. But she quickly stopped smiling when she saw her dad glaring at her. There was nothing that upset her dad more than joking around during class. Alex looked over at her dad and gave him a weak smile. She handed the key back to him. Fun and games would have to wait for later.

Chapter Two

Alex texted with Harper as she kicked back on the big red sofa in the family room. Next to her, Max watched cartoons. Glancing at the TV and then back again to her cell-phone screen, Alex grinned. Everything she needed was within arm's reach. She had all her stuff close by, and she didn't have to get up for anything. Summer was going great.

"Okay," Mrs. Russo said to Justin as they

descended the spiral staircase and headed downstairs. "I think you have everything you need for Wiz Tech. I packed your school uniform—a brand-new wizard robe."

Mr. Russo walked behind them and smiled, remembering his days, many years ago, at Wiz Tech.

"Oh, no, Mom." Justin frowned. "They switched to black bathrobes. The old robes were too formal for these modern, casual times."

Alex couldn't hold back her laughter. Could Justin get *any* geekier? Going to summer school *and* wearing a bathrobe? Please!

Mrs. Russo threw up her hands. "Okay, then. We'll just run out and get you a bathrobe." She grabbed her purse from the side table and headed for the door.

"Ooh!" Mr. Russo followed his wife. "And we should get him some turkey jerky for the long trip."

"Jerry, Justin doesn't like turkey jerky."

She smiled at her husband knowingly. "*You* do."

Mr. Russo shrugged. "Would it hurt us to get a little turkey jerky?" He licked his lips. He knew the salty snack was bad for him, but today was a special occasion. His oldest son was going to Wiz Tech!

Just as Justin and his parents were about to leave, Mrs. Russo stopped and pointed to the wooden floor. "Hey, Alex, you missed a spot right there."

Alex gazed up from her phone, wrinkling her nose in confusion. "What do you mean?"

"It's the only spot in this house that doesn't have your junk all over it," her mom said dryly, gesturing around the room. Alex had to admit her mom was right. Clothes were strewn everywhere. Magazines, nail polish bottles, and hair bands littered the floor. Her pillows and stuffed animals covered the sofa.

"We're taking your brother shopping, and by the time we get back, I expect you to have all your stuff back up in your room," her father instructed.

"Okay." Alex stood and nudged her little brother. "Come on, Max. You've got a lot of cleaning up to do." She clapped her hands to hurry him along. She could usually get Max to do her chores.

"No, no, no, no," Mr. Russo said as he stepped closer to Alex and pointed his finger at her. "Your mess, your responsibility." Then he turned and left with his wife and Justin.

Alex stared at all her things. There had to be almost fifty items to haul upstairs. She sighed in frustration. "Man, getting all this stuff back in my room is going to take forever," she complained. But then she spotted the portal key lying on the table. "Or not," she said slyly.

Alex grabbed the key and raised it above her head. She turned it in the air, and a sparkly gold circle magically shimmered in front of her. "This will be easy. I'll just send my stuff back to my room. *Mailus-spontaneous-Alex-Russo's-bedroom.*" She tossed a pillow in the air and the portal sucked it up. Then she threw a pair of jeans up in the air, and they, too, were transported to her room. Sweet, Alex thought.

"Hey, that thing is kind of like a big vacuum," Max observed.

Her brother was right, Alex realized. Suddenly, she had an idea. "Let me see if I can move it around." She carefully placed her pointer finger inside the golden circle. She took a step to the right and pulled the portal along with her. The magic circle sucked up three of her dirty socks. Alex walked across the room, dragging her vacuum portal with her. Pajamas, magazines, and her hairbrush flew inside. "Awesome. I'll be done in, like, five minutes. Mom and Dad will never—"

Whoosh! In less than a nanosecond, everything in the room disappeared into the portal!

Everything! Alex gazed about in horror. She and Max were standing in completely bare surroundings. No furniture, no floor, no walls—nothing was left at all.

"Um, it's a little cleaner than what I was going for," Alex said nervously, trying to make a joke.

"I'd run away right now, but I don't know where to go," Max said, staring into all the empty space.

Alex bit her lip. "Dad's going to have a cow. And a sheep. And a pig. And a goat when he sees all this." She was used to messing up magic. She had done that more than once before. But this was different. She had never made the entire contents of an *apartment* vanish.

Suddenly, she and Max both heard a key turn in the lock. "Hide!" Alex cried. But where? There was nothing to hide behind! "Oh, never mind."

Their father opened a door that wasn't in

sight and stepped into the blankness. "Boy, I really love this turkey jerky!" he exclaimed, peering into the bag to select just the right piece. "It sure makes me thirsty, though." He walked toward the kitchen, still focused on his bag of turkey jerky. He didn't realize that he was walking into a completely empty room.

But Mrs. Russo and Justin noticed. Both of them stood in the nonexistent doorway, looking into the vacant space in awe.

"Theresa," Mr. Russo called, panic creeping into his voice. "Why can't I open the fridge?" His hand reached for the non-existent handle.

"Because it's not there?" Mrs. Russo guessed. Her eyes darted around in disbelief.

"W-what did you do?" he shrieked, pointing to Alex once he finally noticed everything was missing. Uh-oh, Alex thought. This was bad news. Her dad was really upset!

"I—" Alex decided to tell the truth. "Daddy,

let me just cut to it." She reached into the pocket of her sweatshirt and pulled out the portal key.

"Portal . . . you . . . ahhh!" her father cried. He was too angry to form complete sentences, but Alex got his meaning. She was in trouble.

An hour later, Alex placed the final pillow back on the sofa. "Okay, this is the last of it." Her father had found a spell in one of his ancient magic books and made everything reappear again. Of course, her mess was back to where it had been—all over the place. But this time, Alex didn't complain about cleaning it up the regular way.

Her parents stood together at the kitchen counter, facing the family room. Justin and Max sat on the sofa, but her parents kept their eyes glued on Alex. Her mom shook her head in dismay. "What are we going to do with you, Alex?"

"You have to learn to stop using magic as a shortcut to everything," her father warned. "You are so undisciplined."

"That's why I can't wait to get to Wiz Tech, where everyone is *so* much more serious about magic," Justin noted, coming up behind her. "All summer long, I'll be in classes that focus on the craft of magic and using it *respectfully*, the way it's meant to be. Right, Dad?"

Alex grimaced. Justin was always trying to prove how perfect he was. She glanced at her father to see if he was falling for Justin's act. Her mom and dad smiled and nodded, as if they knew something that no one else did. What's up with them? Alex wondered.

Justin was sensing that something strange was going on, too. "Why are you guys looking at me like I gave you an idea?" he asked nervously.

Oh, no, Alex thought. Were her parents thinking of sending *her* to Wiz Tech, too?

"Please don't tell me he gave you an idea," Alex begged her parents.

"Can someone tell *me* what the idea is?" Max piped up.

Alex put her head in her hands. There was no need to say it out loud. Her summer was going to be *ruined*.

Chapter Three

The next day, Alex found herself staring up at an enormous medieval castle. Gray stone towers and turrets reached high into the cloudless blue sky. A deep moat surrounded the majestic building, and a huge iron door creaked open to let her, Justin, and their parents in.

Inside, the main hall of Wiz Tech was bustling with activity. New students wandered around, their excited chatter echoing off the structure's high ceiling. Flames flickered from golden wall hangings, giving the castle a slightly eerie feel.

Justin entered the room first, his long black robe flowing at his feet. "This is a terrible idea, bringing Alex here to Wiz Tech," he complained. Justin had said this at least a hundred times since yesterday. And, for once, Alex agreed with him.

Mrs. Russo practically had to drag her daughter into the school. "Justin, I know you had your heart set on getting away from your sister, but this could really be good for her." Mrs. Russo glanced at her husband. "And good for all of us."

Oh, please! Alex thought. Mom and Dad are *totally* overreacting. All I did was make our apartment disappear! I mean, it's not like I made the entire city vanish!

"Don't worry, Justin," Mr. Russo told him.

"This is a big place. I'm sure you and Alex will hardly see each other."

"Justin and Alex Russo?" asked a woman wearing a purple velvet cape. She swooped down on them. "I'm Dr. Evilini. You will both be in my class."

Alex eyed their new teacher. Dr. Evilini looked nothing like her teachers back home. Underneath her cape, she wore a rose-colored velvet gown. Long silver earrings dangled from her ears, and perched upon her head was a large purple hat.

Dr. Evilini reached into a burlap sack. "Here are your spectacles." She handed them both a pair.

"Oh, sweet." Justin immediately put on the round, black-framed glasses. "What kind of powers do these glasses give you?" Justin asked.

"None," Dr. Evilini replied. "They just look *wonderful* with black bathrobes."

Alex rolled her eyes. "Great," she mumbled. "We're accessorizing ugly." She turned to her parents and gave them a mournful look. "Mom, Dad, please don't make me stay."

"Yeah. Please don't make her stay," Justin pleaded.

"Come on, guys," their dad said. "The time will fly. Oh, and Justin, here is the portal key." He handed Justin the key. "If you get homesick, just send us a note."

"What about me?" Alex demanded. "Can I use the portal key to send you a note?"

Mr. Russo shook his head. "We've seen enough of you and the portal key."

Alex pouted. There was no way out. She was spending the summer at wizard school.

This is awesome, Max thought, as he walked into the apartment and dropped his skates next to a huge silver kite. No big brother. No big sister. This was going to be a *great* summer.

Just then, he spotted his parents walking down the stairs toward the living room. He listened in quietly.

"Don't worry, honey," Max's dad said to his mother. "Our kids will be fine."

"I'm not worried about *our* kids," Mrs. Russo remarked. "I'm worried about the *other* kids. Alex is there." She gave Mr. Russo a serious look and walked toward the kitchen.

Just then, Mr. Russo looked around the room and noticed a pile of clutter. "Max, what's all this?" his father asked, stepping over all the sports equipment scattered around the family room.

"Well, now that I'm an only child, we can do all that stuff we've been too busy to do. Dad, what do you want to start with?" Max gestured toward a bicycle, some remote-control cars, a scooter, and a giant kayak he'd dragged downstairs from his closet.

"Uh . . ." Mr. Russo's eyes glazed over at the choices. Then he spotted the comfy sofa. "Nap."

"Bike riding around Central Park?" Max suggested.

Mr. Russo sat on the sofa. "A nap."

"Well, how about—" Max started to suggest.

"A nap," his father interrupted, lying down and closing his eyes.

Mrs. Russo had been listening from the kitchen. Frowning, she hurried over to her husband and yanked him upright. "Jerry," she scolded.

"What?" he asked. Then he noticed Max's disappointed face. "Okay. Okay. Max, uh, let's start with what you want to do most," he said.

Max surveyed all of his equipment. Then he reached down and grabbed the sleeping bag. "Camping."

"Camping?" his dad asked, surprised.

His mom laughed. "That's a good one." She

laughed again. "Give me that." She reached for the sleeping bag.

Max held on tightly for a moment, then handed it over to her. Why did his mom think it was funny?

"Oh, come on!" she exclaimed. "You're city guys! Your idea of roughing it is when they deliver Chinese food without the fortune cookies."

"Dad, do you smell that?" Max sniffed the air, a sly grin on his face. "That smells like a challenge."

Mr. Russo sniffed, too. "With a hint of questioning our manhood. You know, we could rough it if we wanted to," he told his wife. "It's just that we don't, because"—he paused to think of a reason—"because there's no wilderness around here."

"We could camp on the terrace," Max suggested, pointing toward the glass sliding door at the back of the apartment.

"Terrace?" Mrs. Russo chuckled.

"Oh, yeah?" Mr. Russo replied, rising to the challenge. "We could spend one—"

"Two," Max interrupted.

"Three nights on the terrace!" Mr. Russo declared.

"Or even a whole week!" Max added.

His dad quickly pulled him aside. "Uh, I think three nights will do it, buddy."

"Okay, campers," Mrs. Russo said. "Three nights on the terrace. You come inside, you lose."

"You are on," Mr. Russo announced.

"Yeah," Max agreed.

Mrs. Russo smiled. "Fine, boys. Enjoy everything Mother Nature has to offer." She tossed the sleeping bag to her husband. The challenge had begun.

That night, long after midnight, Max turned to the left. Then he rolled to the right. He shifted back left, but the wooden slat of the chaise lounge still poked his lower back. And the sleeping bag wasn't padded enough to help. He missed his comfy bed.

Suddenly, bright lights blinded him. Propellers whirred overhead. Both Max and his father gaped up at the shadow of a helicopter hovering directly above!

"You there on the terrace," called a voice from a bullhorn. *"Have you seen a stocky male, late thirties, running with a sack full of money?"*

Max gasped. He had been worried about bugs out on the terrace—not robbers!

"No!" his father called back to the police officer in the helicopter.

"Are you locked out?" the officer called through the bullhorn.

"Yes!" Max and his dad said at the same time. They weren't about to try to start explaining their bet to the officer.

"Hang in there, guys!" The helicopter

whirred away, leaving Max and his dad alone on their terrace. They still had sixty more hours left in the great outdoors. It was going to be a *very* long three days.

Chapter Four

The next morning, Alex was sitting in the back of a classroom, coloring her fingernail with her pen. She hated being at Wiz Tech, surrounded by overachieving wizards. Even worse, she, too, had to wear a black bathrobe and black glasses. If her friends back home ever saw this getup, her fashion cred would be sunk forever.

Dr. Evilini stood at the blackboard, tapping

a picture with a long wooden pointer.

"Anybody?" she asked, scanning the classroom. Justin waved his hand from the front row. "Anybody?" she asked again. She sighed. Justin Russo had answered the last seven questions; his classmates just weren't interested in responding. Dr. Evilini nodded toward Justin.

He beamed and cleared his throat. "Thank you, Dr. Evilini. That would be a *Lithuanian Lethal Lamp*, known for its anaconda-like electrical cords."

Dr. Evilini smiled. "Excellent." She let out an uncontrollable evil laugh. Turning to Justin, she said, "Top-notch, Russo. You really have a grasp on venomous furniture. Don't you agree, class?"

The entire class clapped politely from their old-fashioned wooden desks. "Nice job," a girl near Alex said.

Alex, however, was too busy trying to get a

signal on her cell phone to applaud for her brother. She pressed another button. "What? Only one bar in the wizard world? This stinks!" she complained loudly. She then glanced up to see Dr. Evilini standing in front of her.

"I'll take that," the teacher said crisply.

"Oh. Feel free to add your number so we don't lose touch," Alex joked.

Dr. Evilini snatched the cell phone and returned to the front of the room.

"Yeah, okay," Alex muttered. Wiz Tech was just as bad as Tribeca Prep, Alex thought. She never got away with trying to use her cell phone in any of her classes.

Suddenly, she heard laughter behind her. She whirled around and noticed a boy with curly brown hair and teeny glasses playing with a pocket-sized notebook and the tiny kind of pencil used at minigolf courses.

"What's with you and the tiny stuff?" Alex asked.

"Oh, I come from a family of giants, but I'm kind of the runt of the litter. So, Mom and Dad surround me with miniature things so my self-esteem doesn't get bruised." He held out his hand. "I'm Hugh. Hugh Normous."

"Not really," Alex muttered under her breath.

"Well, that new guy Justin is pretty cool, huh?" Hugh pointed to Alex's brother, who was now proudly straightening the knot on his black-and-gold–striped tie.

"Yeah, the *coolest*," Alex quipped sarcastically. "Watch this." Her eyes sparkled as she ripped a piece of paper from her notebook, folded it, and passed it to a guy sitting on her left.

"Okay." Hugh watched the note as it snaked its way around the classroom toward Justin.

"Not only is it known for its highly venomous vapors, it also engulfs its victims," Dr. Evilini was telling the class. The teacher gazed hopefully at her students for an answer.

Justin raised his hand and chuckled. "Uh, that would be the *Brustromian Beanbag Chair*."

"Impressive, Russo." Dr. Evilini nodded.

Suddenly, Justin felt something tap his left shoulder. He glanced over and quickly caught a note that a girl nearby tossed to him. It had his name on it. Cool, Justin thought. No one at Tribeca Prep had ever passed him a note during class. He unfolded it and—

BOOM!

The note suddenly exploded! Multicolored confetti flew through the air, and Justin's glasses bent from the force of the blast. Then Justin heard Alex's familiar laugh. Justin's face turned bright red. Did his sister *always* have to embarrass him?

Dr. Evilini reached for the remains of the note and read it aloud. "*Love, Alex.*"

"Yeah!" Alex raised her arm in victory. She giggled again. Finally, my day is getting interesting, she thought to herself smugly.

But Dr. Evilini wasn't laughing. At all. In fact, she looked really angry. She walked over to Alex's desk. "Miss Russo, I get the feeling you are too undisciplined to appreciate what Wiz Tech has to offer."

"And I get the feeling that you people here at Wiz Tech don't get *me*," Alex replied.

"Perhaps this will get your attention," Dr. Evilini said, handing Alex two dirty blackboard erasers. Alex looked at her teacher and sighed. She knew what that meant. Detention.

After school had ended, Alex gathered the dirty erasers to begin clapping them. But these weren't ordinary erasers: a zooming letter suddenly flew out of one! Alex dodged the letter as it hurtled toward her head.

"Whoa!" She leaned against the blackboard and more warily clapped the two erasers together. But instead of chalk dust, more letters flew out. Ps, Gs, and Qs swarmed around her head. Bs, Ls, and Ws dove dangerously close to her elbows. She ducked as a K dive-bombed her. Then a J lodged right into her lip. "Ow! Those Js are like fishhooks."

Dr. Evilini's eyes glinted as she watched Alex attempt to finish clapping the erasers. "Summer's just begun, Russo," she warned.

After Alex had finished her after-school punishment, she wove her way through the students gathered in the main hall. "Hey, Justin!" she called to her brother. "How'd you like my exploding note? I thought it was a blast." She laughed at her own joke.

"Well, no one else did," Justin told her. "Messing with me didn't turn out like you thought, did it?" He narrowed his eyes and gave his sister a long stare. "Everyone around here thinks I'm cool, and they think *you're* a loser," he declared confidently.

"A *loser*?" Alex asked incredulously. "What

are you talking about? People love hanging out with me." She turned to the kids hurrying past her to the dining hall. "Hey, who wants to have lunch with me?"

All the kids booed.

Justin tried to hide his excitement. Finally, he thought to himself. *Finally*, I'm more popular than Alex. I'm staying at Wiz Tech forever, Justin decided.

Hugh, meanwhile, moved toward Alex. "I'll have lunch with you," he offered. "I hope you like baby corn, baby carrots, and tiny mugs of juice." He gestured to his mini lunch box.

Justin snickered. "Yeah, have fun with the really tiny giant." He turned and headed up the wide marble staircase leading to the classrooms upstairs.

"Oh, yeah!" Alex sputtered. "Well, let's see how big man on campus fits in with this." She raised her arm and recited: "*From your chin to your toes, an elephant trunk grows.*" She sent sparks flying toward Justin.

But at the moment the magic was about to strike Justin, Dr. Evilini crossed his path. "Russo!" she cried. An elephant's trunk appeared in the middle of *her* face instead.

Alex cringed. "Um, that wasn't really meant for you." She tried to back away. "Sorry."

Zap! Metal bars instantly clanked down around Alex. Dr. Evilini had trapped her—right in the middle of the main hall—in a cage!

"But *this* is clearly meant for me," Alex said with a sigh as all the kids gawked at her. Dr. Evilini magically removed her elephant trunk and glared in Alex's direction.

Guess we're not going to have that special student-teacher relationship, Alex thought. Could this day get any worse?

Later that afternoon, Hugh crawled through a tiny door and entered a circular room in the castle's farthest tower. "I've summoned Justin Russo as you've requested, Dr. Evilini."

The teacher nodded and then shooed Hugh away. He ducked back through the small door as Justin entered through a normal-sized door beside it.

Justin cleared his throat. "Uh, you wanted to see me?"

Dr. Evilini spun around. She stood in front of what appeared to be a five-sided Ping-Pong table. "Yes." She pointed to a double-sided paddle lying on one section of the table. "Pick up that Bidaddle."

Justin looked at his teacher curiously and lifted the paddle. The handle was in the middle, and jutting out from both ends were Ping-Pong paddles. He held it like a baton. "Uh, why?" he asked.

But there was no more time for questions. Small gold balls began to fly rapidly at him. He swatted at them furiously. Justin returned them—moving quickly to his left, his right, and then to his left again. He was out of breath when the barrage of balls stopped.

Dr. Evilini grinned.

"What?" Justin demanded.

"Just as I thought. It has been written that great twelve-ball players turn into great wizards. And you might be one." She broke out into an evil laugh. Then she cleared her throat. "What were we talking about?"

"Twelve-ball. What's twelve-ball?" he asked. "It looks like Ping-Pong."

"Oh, it's nothing like Ping-Pong." She held up a gold ball. "These balls are added one by one with the objective of twelve being played simultaneously. Only one student has ever reached eleven balls here at Wiz Tech."

"Who's that?" Justin asked.

"Jerko Phoenix. You'll meet him. In due time, my boy, in due time." She cackled. Then she turned to Justin. "What do you say? Are you up to it?"

Justin nodded eagerly. "I am. I am up to the challenge." He tried out his most evil laugh, hoping to sound like his teacher, but he ended up coughing and sputtering instead. "I'm going to get some water," he choked. I definitely need to practice that, he thought. That didn't sound evil at all.

Instead, he spent the next several hours practicing twelve-ball. He was really getting good at it!

Dr. Evilini definitely took training Justin seriously. She taught Justin correct Bidaddle techniques and twelve-ball strategy. She focused on his footwork, his paddle rhythm, and his spin serve. He was panting even before she called in four other students for a match. He was more used to studying than he was playing any type of sport.

But Justin wasn't about to take a break

now. He grabbed a black sweater with a white number nine on the front and pulled it over his head. He stood by his side of the table holding a Bidaddle in each hand. The other players positioned themselves by each of the four remaining sides. There was now a crowd watching, including Alex and Hugh. Dr. Evilini threw the first ball in. Then the second. Then the third and the fourth. Gold balls kept coming at him furiously.

Justin smacked the balls at a dizzying pace. Bounce, hit. Bounce, hit. The rhythm flowed through his body. He hit the balls faster and harder. Twirling his Bidaddle, he slammed a ball toward one of his opponents, knocking him to the ground and out of the game. The balls moved even faster now, and Justin continued picking up speed. He blocked the gold balls, one after the other after the other. He slammed the ball again and again, flooring two more opponents. Now it was Justin against one last opponent, number seven. But he hit the ball again, and number seven was out of the game.

Justin reached for a towel to wipe the sweat from his face. He shook hands with the other kids. Who knew that winning in sports could be so exhilarating? It felt as good as winning the science fair, he decided.

From the sidelines, Hugh watched in amazement. "He's the best I've ever seen," he told Alex.

Alex huffed. "You're the worst best friend *ever*." She'd had enough of watching Justin get all the attention. She hurried away.

"Wait up, Alex!" Hugh cried, chasing after her.

Dr. Evilini pulled Justin aside. "Mr. Russo, it's time for you to take on the very best twelve-ball player here at Wiz Tech in a non-binding scrimmage." She pulled her wand from her cape and sent a fire bolt toward the door.

Justin waited anxiously. Then someone tapped him on the shoulder.

He turned to see a tall guy standing next to him—with brown hair, a square jaw, and piercing blue eyes. Actually, a piercing blue *eye*. His right eye was covered with a black patch.

Dr. Evilini smiled. "Justin Russo, meet—"

"Jerko Phoenix," the boy interrupted.

"Jerko? Oh, that must be a tough name to grow up with. You know, I had a cousin whose name was Kim. Well, uh, Kim was a guy, so I'm sure you can imagine people—" Justin stammered nervously.

"Enough," Jerko interrupted again. "I'm here to warn you I plan on winning the title of 'Mr. Twelve-Ball,'" he declared with a smirk.

Justin decided not to take the bait. "What's up with your eye?" he asked instead. "Twelve-ball accident?"

Jerko sniffed. "There's nothing wrong with my eye." He lifted the eye patch and slid it over his left eye. "This gets me out of wearing those stupid glasses." Then he slid the patch back over his right eye.

What a phony! Justin thought. He adjusted his glasses. He happened to like them. And he liked twelve-ball. This Jerko dude better keep both eyes wide open when he plays me, Justin thought. Because I am *good* at twelve-ball. Really good.

Chapter Five

Max and his dad had been terrace camping for two days, and Max was bored. Out-of-his-mind, antsy bored. So far, they hadn't really done anything outdoorsy, except for, well, being outside.

Max and his dad spent the morning playing card games. Max wondered if this was what real camping was like. Probably not. Real camping was fishing in a stream, hiking in the woods, and roasting marshmallows by a campfire. Real camping was being out in *nature*. City camping was sitting on deck furniture on a concrete terrace playing games as the broiling sun bore down on you and exhaust fumes from buses wafted up from the street.

"Got any fours?" Max asked his dad.

"Go fish," his dad told Max before studying his own cards. "You got any twos?"

"Go fish," Max said.

At that moment, a pigeon flew overhead, dropping a not-so-pleasant surprise down on them.

"I'm not fishing in that pond!" Mr. Russo exclaimed, throwing down his cards.

Max groaned. He was hoping for nature—but this isn't what he had in mind!

That night was even worse. Max huddled beside his father under a vinyl tablecloth. Cold rain poured down on them. They had tried to create a tent by draping the tablecloth over two chairs. But the tablecloth was a poor excuse for a roof, and they were drenched. Max's jeans stuck to his legs, and his shirt was soaked. The black garbage bags they were wearing over their clothes were lousy substitutes for raincoats. Max brushed his wet bangs out of his eyes.

Mr. Russo reached over and handed him a soggy dandelion. They had eaten up all their supply of turkey jerky and chips earlier that afternoon. Max pushed it away, even though he was starving. He knew fancy restaurants put dandelions in salads, but he wasn't *that* hungry. Yet.

For what must've been the tenth time, Mrs. Russo peeked out of the apartment window. She sighed and gazed around the warm, cozy family room. Finally, she threw up her arms and hurried to the kitchen. "It's been raining all night, and they're eating weeds again.

That's it. Game over," she said aloud.

She opened the refrigerator, grabbed a potato, and stuck a thin, black pen into it. Then she poked two yellow corn-cob holders on top. She surveyed her work. Not great, but she didn't have time for major arts and crafts. It would have to do.

She walked over to the sofa, bent down, and shoved the decorated spud underneath. Now it was time for a little drama.

She screamed. Loudly.

"Help! Max! Jerry! Help!" she shrieked.

The glass door to the terrace slid open, and her husband and son rushed into the apartment. "Mom, are you all right?" Max asked, hurrying to her side.

"What happened?" Mr. Russo cried.

Mrs. Russo's eyes widened. "I saw a rat. It's under the couch."

"A rat?" gasped her husband. Then he raced back to the safety of the terrace; Max was only steps behind him. If it's one thing they were both scared of, it was rodents.

Mrs. Russo sighed. She was going to have to act really terrified. "You guys! Help, *now*!"

Her husband dashed back into the living room. This time, he held a pair of barbecue tongs as a weapon. He wasn't about to try to capture the rat with his bare hands.

"It's, uh . . ." He stared uncertainly at the sofa. "Uh . . . It's under the, uh . . . ?" He motioned toward the couch.

"Uh-huh," Mrs. Russo answered.

Mr. Russo crouched down and stared under the sofa, holding on tightly to the pair of tongs. "Okay." He gasped when he caught sight of the object. Then he slowly stood up and scratched his head. "The tail looks like—"

"A rat," Theresa interrupted her husband, before he could figure out her trick. "Jerry, it's a rat," she said adamantly.

"Oh." He still looked confused. Something

about the rat just didn't seem right.

"That's it!" Mrs. Russo declared. "You guys can't stay out there anymore. You guys win. I need you in here." She gave her husband a knowing look.

Suddenly, Mr. Russo understood. This was all a trick to end the camping trip. He smiled and squeezed her shoulder gently. "Thanks," he whispered. He turned to his son. "Max, camping trip is over." He leaned down and snatched up the potato in a garbage bag. "Uh, I've got to put this little guy back in his natural habitat—the subway," he told Max. He quickly headed out of the apartment.

Max didn't quite believe his parents' story. "Hey, Mom. That was really a potato, wasn't it?" he commented. "Yeah," she admitted. Oh, no, Mrs. Russo thought to herself. What if Max had realized he'd been duped and wanted to go back outside again? she worried.

"Do you have any more?" he asked, pulling

off his dripping garbage bag. He was so happy to be in his warm, dry home. "Because I'm *starving*."

Mrs. Russo smiled. Her plan had worked! "Sure. How do you want your rat? Mashed or fried?"

Chapter Six

Alex glanced down the darkened hallway. Totally empty. Perfect!

Now was the time.

She grabbed the handle of her pink rolling suitcase and jogged down the corridor. Her sneakers squeaked on the marble at the top of the wide staircase leading down to the main hall. She glanced around. She was still alone.

But for how long? She had to get out of there *now*.

She raced down the stairs, dragging her suitcase behind her. *Thump, thump.* The wheels whacked loudly against each stair, announcing her escape plan. "Shh!" she whispered to her suitcase as she picked up speed. Freedom was only a few feet away.

She ran to the huge wooden door. There were two metal chains bolting it shut. She tugged at the knob. The heavy door wouldn't budge.

She sighed. This was the third door in the school she had tried. "This door is locked, too?" she muttered to herself.

The chains opened and closed like a mouth. "Yes, I am," answered the door.

Alex stared at the door and sighed. This school is so weird, she thought to herself. I have to get out of here!

Suddenly, Alex heard a voice behind her.

"Alex, what are you doing? It's bath night."
Alex turned around to see Justin wearing a plaid bathrobe. He had a towel slung over his shoulder and was holding a bar of soap.

"Oh, just chitchatting with the door," she replied, trying to sound casual. "Um, hey, Justin, you know the portal key Dad gave you? I need it. I want to send something home."

"Oh. Okay." He reached into his robe pocket for the key. Then he noticed that she wasn't wearing her school uniform, and that she was carrying her luggage. "Wait," he said, eyeing her suspiciously. "Why do you have your suitcase?"

"Um, I just want Mom to do some laundry for me," she fibbed.

"Hey!" he exclaimed. His detective skills finally kicked into gear. "You're trying to send yourself home."

"Okay. So? What do you care?" Alex challenged. "You love all the work at this place.

I can't stand it." She grabbed the key out of Justin's hand. She was desperate. "I'm out of here."

"Alex, you can't leave," Justin warned.

"Oh, yeah? Watch me." She turned the key in midair, opening the golden portal. *"Mailus-spontaneous-Russo-home."*

In an instant, she was sucked into the portal. She closed her eyes, and her body hurtled at intense speed through a wind tunnel. Her ears popped from the force. Then she heard voices.

"Here, Hugh," Dr. Evilini was saying. "I do appreciate the help with the mail."

"Oh, you're welcome," Hugh replied. "But it's a little lonely. I wish my new friend Alex would drop by once in a while."

Suddenly, Alex hit the ground with a thud. She opened her eyes . . .

And saw that she was in Dr. Evilini's office!

"Hey, everybody!" Alex exclaimed, trying to act cool.

It was the last day of school, and Alex was psyched. That is, until Justin came over and tried to embarrass her, as usual.

Alex decided to use magic so it wouldn't take her hours to clean up the mess she had made in the living room.

When Mr. and Mrs. Russo saw that Alex's attempts at magic had caused everything in the house to disappear, they decided she would join Justin at Wiz Tech for the summer.

Alex and Justin couldn't believe the news!

"This is a big place. I'm sure you and Alex will hardly see each other," Mr. Russo told Justin when he and Alex arrived at Wiz Tech.

Justin was having a blast at wizard school. And he was a whiz when it came to playing twelve-ball, the coolest sport at school.

Dr. Evilini made Alex clap erasers as punishment for disrupting class. But instead of chalk dust, letters flew out of the erasers!

Max and his dad's outdoor camping trip on the terrace didn't go quite as planned.

When Mr. Russo and Max heard Mrs. Russo scream,
they came running inside to investigate. She told
them that she had spotted a rat!

Mrs. Russo's plan to get Max and Mr. Russo to
come inside had worked!

"Now go get those customers!" Mr. Russo exclaimed to Max, who was dressed up in a giant sandwich costume.

Justin realized that Alex was telling the truth—Dr. Evilini really *was* trying to drain his powers!

While Mr. and Mrs. Russo wanted Justin to win the twelve-ball match, Alex was hoping that he would lose!

Don't hit the ball, Alex thought to herself.

Alex decided to try and help Justin keep his magical powers. "Some are evil, some are kind. But now all must speak their mind," Alex chanted to Dr. Evilini.

Mr. and Mrs. Russo couldn't believe that Dr. Evilini had just revealed her plan to take Justin to Volcanoland!

"Alex!" Hugh cried, dropping the envelopes he was holding to rush over to her.

"Alex!" Justin echoed as he hurried through the office door moments later. "All mail goes through Dr. Evilini." He saw Alex's disappointed look. "I guess you know that now."

Dr. Evilini strolled over to her, clasping her hands together with glee. "Alex Russo. Trying to run away instead of facing up to the challenges of Wiz Tech. I can see I'm going to have to pull the old discipline bucket."

"The *who*?" Alex asked.

Minutes later, Alex found herself on her hands and knees, scrubbing the grimy hallway floor with a toothbrush. *Her* toothbrush! She dipped it in a wooden bucket filled with soapy water. Across the bucket was the word DISCIPLINE.

"She wasn't kidding," Alex grumbled. "There really *is* a discipline bucket. I hate this place." She was already beginning to plot her next escape attempt.

The main door chuckled as she worked nearby. "Keep scrubbing," the door taunted through its chain-linked lips.

All of these talking doors were so creepy! Alex reminded herself to slam the door as hard as she could tomorrow.

Then she heard Dr. Evilini's voice at the top of the stairs. Alex groaned. She'd had enough of her teacher for one night.

"Are you sure you got the message?" Dr. Evilini asked.

Alex looked at her strangely. Dr. Evilini was holding a small white, orange, and black fish.

"Yes," the fish replied.

Alex squinted in disbelief. Was that really a talking *fish*?

"Good. Then take it straight to my mother," Dr. Evilini instructed it. "She'll finally be proud of me. Now, go, messenger fish. Flop like the wind!" She released the fish and headed back toward her office.

"Ow, ow, ow, ow, ow, ow, ow, ow, ow," cried the fish, as it flopped down stair after stair. It landed alongside Alex's bucket.

"Hey, I just scrubbed there!" Alex exclaimed as she grabbed a hold of the messenger fish.

The fish began to speak. "'Dear Mama, after the twelve-ball tournament reveals the best young wizard, I will drain that wizard's powers and take them for myself, making me the most powerful wizard ever. Love, Mary Beth Evilini.'"

Alex stared at the fish in shock. "Justin's going to get his powers drained?"

The door hummed a foreboding tune—one that promised doom ahead.

Alex frowned at the door. "This place is a freak show."

She realized now that she wasn't going home anytime soon. She had no choice. She had to stay at Wiz Tech and help protect Justin.

"Did my messenger fish just tell you my evil

plan?" said Dr. Evilini, who had hurried down the stairs and now glared accusingly at Alex.

"No," Alex fibbed.

The fish looked annoyed.

"All right. This time, pay attention," the fish instructed Alex. "'Dear Mama, you'll be proud to know that after the twelve-ball tournament reveals the best young wizard, I will drain—'"

Alex clapped her hand over the fish's mouth. She blushed. She was so busted. "Okay, maybe he did tell me," Alex admitted.

"Hey, at least I didn't tell her about Volcanoland," the fish said defensively.

"I never said anything about Volcanoland!" Dr. Evilini exclaimed.

"Well, you have to go to an undersea volcano to drain a wizard's powers," the messenger fish explained. "And Volcanoland is the only—"

Dr. Evilini snatched the tattling fish from Alex and tossed it in the bucket of soapy water. But her secret was out. Dr. Evilini stepped closer to Alex. "We have a problem," she said. "You just heard my plan."

"And I *love* your plan," Alex insisted. She glanced around the dark room. She was alone. It was better not to make Dr. Evilini any angrier. "I think it'd be great for me if Justin wins the tournament, and you drain his powers." She nodded enthusiastically.

"How so?" Dr. Evilini asked suspiciously.

Alex's brain zoomed into overdrive. "Because without his powers"—she thought fast— "there's no way he'll end up being the family wizard. I will. Well, of course, there's Max, but he thinks microwave popcorn's magic, so . . ."

"Hmm." Dr. Evilini gazed at Alex thoughtfully. She seemed to like Alex's reasoning. "Well, it looks like we are on the same side. Care to seal it with a laugh?"

"I'll try," Alex said, letting out her scariest laugh.

Dr. Evilini shook her head. "It needs more

bass." She opened her mouth and let out an evil, wicked, chill-down-the-spine laugh.

"I thought I heard voices," said a man in a flowing black silk robe who had shuffled into the hall. His long, white beard almost touched his knees. He was holding a blueberry muffin.

Dr. Evilini straightened up. "Good evening, Headmaster Crumbs," she greeted the director of the school in a sickly sweet voice. "Just here with one of my prized students."

Headmaster Crumbs squinted. "Really? *Alex Russo* is one of your prized students? All of the other teachers say she's remarkably slack. And you know how we feel about slackers. We don't like slackers."

Dr. Evilini draped her arm around Alex's shoulder. "Perhaps they don't know Miss Russo as well as I do."

Headmaster Crumbs took a large bite of his muffin. "Well, then perhaps I should stick around and get to know you, too." He took a step closer. "Now, what are we talking about?"

Alex felt trapped. Evil teacher on one side. Weird guy with a muffin on the other side. "Uh, just girl talk," she told the headmaster.

"Oh, well then," he replied. "I've got to go."

Alex exhaled with relief. She had to get out of there, too. She needed to warn Justin!

Chapter Seven

Max wiped a damp rag over the top of a table at the Waverly Sub Station. With Justin and Alex away at Wiz Tech, his parents had asked him to help out more at the restaurant. But Max didn't mind. His dad said he'd split all the tips with him. And Max had had enough of outdoor adventures for a while. He'd been saving all of his money to buy the newest video game and spend the rest of the summer on the sofa, remote control in one hand, a bag of pretzels in the other.

He glanced around the restaurant. The place was designed to look like an old subway station, with blue and white tiles and subway signs hanging on the walls. It was usually packed with customers, but at the moment the restaurant was almost completely empty. How am I supposed to save up for a video game if no one is around to tip me? Max wondered.

Then he heard a high-pitched, female voice right outside the restaurant door. "Forget the Waverly Sub Station, they use day-old bread. Beautiful people eat at The Salad Bowl!" She practically sang out the name of the vegetarian establishment down the block.

Max hurried to the window and peered through the glass. He couldn't believe his eyes. A woman dressed in a salad bowl costume was standing in front of the Sub Station! Her face poked out of a hole in a piece of green foam shaped like a lettuce leaf.

"Lots of attractive women eat salad these days," she said to a man at the corner. She handed him a flyer. The guy smiled and headed down the street—toward The Salad Bowl. Max frowned. What was going on here?

Suddenly, Mrs. Russo flung open the front door of the Sub Station. Max and his father hurried behind her. "Look at this!" she exclaimed. "No wonder we had such a slow day." She walked over to the woman in the salad-bowl costume. "Excuse me. What do you think you're doing? It's not Halloween, and you're too old to be trick-or-treating anyway."

"Listen," Mr. Russo added. "If you don't mind, why don't you stand in front of the clown supply? I think you fit in better over there."

The woman in the costume smirked. "I have to stand here, because I'm stealing your customers with my crisp lettuce and crunchy cucumbers."

"You can't do that!" Max protested.

"That's what the hot-dog guy in Washington Square Park said," she reported gleefully. "Now he's the guy holding the arrow pointing toward CHEAP FURNITURE GOING OUT OF BUSINESS." She stepped toward Max, her smile morphing into a vicious sneer. "So, back off!"

"Listen, you talking bowl of freak!" shouted Mrs. Russo, who reached out both arms to tear a tomato from her rival's costume.

Just then, Mr. Russo stepped in. "You are *not* going to steal our customers," he warned. "Submarine sandwiches have a long history in New York City. I know New Yorkers, and New Yorkers love sandwiches. They're not going to give them up for tomatoes, carrots"—he peered at her costume—"and what are those? *Snails?*"

Salad Bowl Girl scoffed. "They're porcini mushrooms."

Mr. Russo's eyes lit up. "Oh, I love porcini mushrooms!"

Max sighed. Mention food and his dad became completely preoccupied.

"Jerry! Get inside!" his mom called.

Mr. Russo blushed and followed his wife and son back into the Sub Station. He took a deep breath. "Okay," he told them. "All we have to do is advertise our shop like she advertises hers."

"Where are we going to find a goof to wear a ridiculous costume for us?" Max asked.

Mrs. Russo let out a small gasp. She smiled at her husband, and then they both stared at Max. Max knew he was doomed.

The next afternoon, Mrs. Russo peered out the front door. Waverly Place was bustling with people on their lunch hour doing errands and looking for a place to grab lunch. She pointed to the woman in the salad-bowl costume, who was back handing out flyers.

Mr. Russo stepped onto the sidewalk. "Hmm." He narrowed his eyes. "Go get her, Max." He looked behind him. Where was his son? "Max!" he called.

Max waddled through the door. The foam submarine-sandwich costume his parents had created covered him from head to toe! He stepped into the fresh air and sniffed. "Hey, how did you get it to smell like onions?" Max asked.

His mom leaned in, inhaled, and wrinkled her nose. "Oh, that's you," she told Max. She then turned to her husband. "Jerry, it needs more ventilation holes."

"That's why we went with the Swiss cheese," he said. He placed both hands on the foam bread that covered Max's shoulders and gave him a reassuring glance. "Now go get those customers!"

"Yeah," Max said grimly.

His dad looked over at him. While he knew

it wasn't the coolest thing in the world to be dressed as a giant sandwich, it would really boost sales for the restaurant. Mr. Russo gave him an encouraging pat on the back.

Suddenly Max lost his balance and fell face-first onto the sidewalk! It was hard to stand up in a foam-sandwich suit.

"Are you okay?" his mom cried.

Max smiled weakly. His dad helped lift him to his feet. He was fine, but he *was not* excited about being dressed in this costume. He brushed the dust off his foam cheese and bologna outfit, and cleared his throat. "Get your Bronxstrami! Central Pork Sandwich! Right here at the Sub Station!" he shouted, trying to sound enthusiastic. "Mmmm."

Two men and one woman smiled at Max and headed into the restaurant.

"Hey, it's working!" Mr. Russo exclaimed.

Mrs. Russo pinched Max's cheek. "That's my boy."

The woman in the salad costume then appeared at Max's side. "Salads make you perky," she called to a woman about to enter the Sub Station. "Sandwiches make you sleepy."

Max chuckled. "You know why people eat salads with a roll? Because it makes a sandwich in their stomachs!"

The woman laughed and entered his family's restaurant. Score another one for Max!

The woman in the salad costume was starting to become frustrated. "You—you have to eat sandwiches with your hands!" she shouted. "Like *savages*."

Max rolled his eyes and tried to think of a clever comeback. Just then, two more customers walked into his family's sandwich shop.

"All right, you won this lunch rush," the costumed woman conceded. "But if you're here tomorrow, you're going to get it."

"Ooh, I am scared of lettuce. It's high in vitamins and fiber. Oooh!" Max teased her, pretending to be frightened. But he was pumped. A few more days of this and the Waverly Sub Station will prevail, he thought. Bring it on!

Chapter Eight

"It's time for the serve-and-volley drill," Jerko Phoenix instructed Justin. They were practicing in the twelve-ball room. "You serve. I volley. You cry for mercy." He twirled his Bidaddle confidently.

Suddenly Jerko's eyes widened. A pretty girl had just walked into the room. He stared in her direction and smiled. Suddenly, a barrage of little gold balls bounced off of him.

"I wasn't ready!" he sputtered to Justin. The girl had distracted him. But it wasn't just any girl. It was Alex.

"Uh, Justin." Alex smiled apologetically at Jerko. "Can I talk to you?"

"I kind of need to practice. I'm playing in the semifinals tomorrow," Justin said.

Alex pulled her brother away, while Jerko, in a black sweater boasting the number one, showed off his spin serve. "No, you're not," she told Justin. "Dr. Evilini is going to drain the twelve-ball champion's powers at Volcanoland. I can't let you win this thing."

"I'm sorry," Justin responded in confusion. "Volcano-*what*?"

"Her messenger fish told me," Alex explained. "She wants to become the most powerful wizard ever."

"So, there's a volcano *and* a messenger fish?" he asked. Oh, boy, Justin thought to himself. His sister had *finally* lost it.

"We need to focus on Evilini!" Alex cried. She had to make Justin understand how important this was. "I don't know if you know, but she's *evil*."

"No," Justin said slowly. "Her *name* is Evilini."

"And how much clearer could it be?" Alex asked. Didn't Justin get it?

"Okay, if she were *really* evil, don't you think she would have changed her name to Really-Friendly-*ini*, or Nice-*ini*, or Totally-Not-Evil-*ini*?" he pointed out.

Alex gritted her teeth. "All right, we're not getting anywhere! You need to listen to me!" she pleaded.

"This is exactly why I didn't want you to come to Wiz Tech," he explained. "Stop bothering me. I need to focus and concentrate." He turned back to the twelve-ball table—and was smacked in the head by seven of Jerko's killer serves.

"If I could focus, I would have hit those!" Justin exclaimed defensively. He twirled his Bidaddle, ready for the next round of balls that were coming his way.

Alex knew Justin was never going to listen to her. She needed help. *Official* help. She raced into Headmaster Crumbs's classroom.

"Headmaster Crumbs, I need your help," she said breathlessly.

"What seems to be the problem?" he asked.

"Dr. Evilini is going to drain the twelve-ball champion's powers at Volcanoland. And I think my brother may end up champion!" she exclaimed. "You have to do something!"

Headmaster Crumbs shook his head sadly. "I can't. My hands are tied."

Alex sighed. "You don't believe me, either?"

"No, my hands are really tied." He lifted his arms and showed Alex the rope tied around both wrists. "I lost a bet with Evilini. Professor Maloney and I got into a beard contest of which I had no business being part of." He looked down at the beard that reached past his knees. Apparently Professor Maloney's beard was even longer.

"Don't you see?" Alex urged. "That bet was a setup! Evilini has tied your hands so you can't do anything about her plan!" she cried.

"You may be on to something," Headmaster Crumbs replied. "But I can't confront Evilini. She'd only deny it. If you want to protect Justin, it's up to you. Get him to back out of the tournament."

"I already tried," Alex explained. "But once I mentioned Volcanoland and the talking fish, he thought I was messing with him."

"Hmm." The headmaster stood up and paced the room, deep in thought. "Sounds like you need some hard evidence to convince your brother. I suggest you go to the library."

"Sure, I'll go to the library," Alex said in

defeat. She headed toward the door with a heavy sigh. This was no help. She'd have to figure out something else.

Headmaster Crumbs looked at Alex and raised his bushy white eyebrows. "Oh, really? Is that the truth?"

Alex turned around. "Sure," Alex fibbed. She'd learned long ago that teachers loved it if you said you were going to the library. Something about all those books, she guessed.

"*Some are evil, some are kind. But now all must speak their mind*," chanted the headmaster. He raised his arm and zapped Alex with a bolt of blue light.

"I hate libraries." Alex jumped back, startled that she had just spoken. "What am I saying? There's no way I'm going to a library." Alex gasped. It was like her mouth was on autopilot!

"I put a truth spell on you to see if you are really on your way to help Justin, or if you're just going to slack off again," he explained.

Alex exhaled. Magic! That explained it. "I want to help, but not at a boring library," she admitted.

"Well, then go some place where it isn't boring. Like Volcanoland," he suggested.

"How do I get to Volcanoland?" Alex asked.

"I can't tell you that." Headmaster Crumbs shuffled back to his desk.

"Then why'd you just tell me to go there?' Alex demanded.

"I didn't," he said. "I would never say that." He nodded his head up and down. "I'm the headmaster. I can't send a student off-campus to Volcanoland." He nodded again.

"What?" Why was he nodding *yes* at the same time he was telling her she wasn't allowed to go? Alex was more confused than ever. Wiz Tech is getting more and more strange by the day, Alex thought to herself.

"You should *never* go to Volcanoland," he instructed, still nodding. "It could be dangerous."

Wait! Maybe this was some kind of code, Alex realized. Maybe he thought Evilini was listening in or something. "So just to be clear," Alex said slowly, "you want me to go to Volcanoland."

The headmaster nodded vigorously. "I didn't say that."

Alex thought she got his signal, but she wanted to be extra sure. "But you did say Volcanoland."

He smiled and winked. "I will admit to that."

Okay, then. She was going to Volcanoland.

But first she had to check on Justin and Dr. Evilini. She was afraid to leave them together for too long. She pushed through a crowd of cheering students who had now gathered in the twelve-ball room. She spotted Justin sitting in the bleachers on one of the five sides of the table. The other four sides were defended by guys she didn't know. Balls zoomed through the air at the speed of light.

"What's happening?" she asked Hugh, who was standing next to her.

"Justin's fallen behind," he reported.

"Oh, good. Maybe I don't have to go to Volcanoland." She leaned closer for a better view.

"The only way he can win now is if he hits the tattler," Hugh explained.

"The tattler?" Alex asked.

"Yeah, it's an obscure rule," Hugh replied. "If you hit the tattler, it's an automatic win. But the tattler isn't even here, so there's no chance." Hugh's eyes suddenly widened. "There she is!" he cried.

Alex followed his gaze to the side of the room. A little girl with blond curls wearing a frilly, white party dress whispered something into the ear of a Wiz Tech teacher. "What's she doing?"

"She's tattling. She's the tattler. It's obvious," Hugh said.

At that very moment, a gold ball ricocheted off Justin's Bidaddle. It soared across the room, smacking the tattler in the arm.

"He did it!" Hugh yelled. The crowd was on its feet, cheering. "He hit the tattler!"

Justin jumped, pumping his fists into the air. "I won! I'm going to the finals!" He could barely contain his excitement. Sure, he had won academic competitions, but to win a sports game? It was completely different—and awesome!

Dr. Evilini grinned. "Well played, Russo. It's now down to you and Jerko. We'll soon find out who's the most powerful young wizard."

An evil laugh suddenly rang out. "Oh, sorry. My cell phone." Dr. Evilini reached into the pocket of her purple robe and pulled out a small silver phone. Flipping it open, she answered in a syrupy voice, "Hello, Mummy?"

Alex looked from Dr. Evilini to Justin. "I've got to get to Volcanoland," she said seriously. Time was running out. If she didn't hurry, Justin would be drained of his magical powers—forever!

Chapter Nine

Justin walked through the crowded main hall of Wiz Tech. Kids high-fived him. Girls pointed to him and whispered to their friends. He was now superpopular. And he was loving it.

He looked around for Alex. He wanted her to witness his newly gained popularity. She would be so proud of him! But he couldn't find her anywhere.

Just then, Jerko approached. "I guess it's just you, me, and destiny," he told Justin.

Justin wrinkled his forehead in confusion. "No, Destiny Johnson lost in the third round," he said.

Jerko laughed. "No. Destiny, as in 'it's my destiny to be a winner and your destiny to always live in my shadow.'"

"Well, I'll see you in the finals," Justin said.

Meanwhile, Alex was still in the bleachers with Hugh. She'd been trying to figure out a way to escape from school, and she couldn't come up with anything. "How am I going to get to Volcanoland?" she asked him. "I'd mail myself, but all the mail goes through Dr. Evilini and she's evil."

"I work in the mail room," Hugh replied. "I can get around Evilini."

Alex stared at Hugh in amazement. "Are you saying you could mail me from the mail room without Evilini knowing?"

"I'm not saying that at all," he said. Then he nodded again and again.

"What is it with you people and your head-nodding?" Alex asked in frustration. But she finally understood. Hugh was really saying he'd do it! Alex was ecstatic. There was still a chance she could save Justin!

A short time later, Alex touched down in Volcanoland. She quickly found her way to the information desk.

"Excuse me," she said to the lady, who stood there with a bored look on her face. Her brown hair was styled in an unflattering bowl cut, and she was wearing a navy uniform with a lot of gold buttons and fringes along the shoulders. "I need some information on the volcano."

"Fire away," the woman replied in a low, raspy voice. "We're encouraged to use volcano terminology whenever we can," she confided.

"Is it true the volcano can drain wizards of their powers?" Alex asked.

"The majority of wizards enjoy the natural

wonder of the park and take a lot of pictures that they'll bore their friends with when they get home," she recited.

"What about the others?" Alex pressed.

"Oh, they use the volcano to drain wizards of their powers," she whispered. "That's a separate entrance fee."

"I have to prove this to my brother before it's too late," Alex explained. But she knew that Justin wouldn't be easily convinced. "Hey, could you come back to school with me?"

"What for?" the woman asked. "You got something bubbling?" She chuckled at her pun. "See what I did there?"

"You're a volcano official. My brother always believes people in uniform," Alex told her. "It's one of the many things about him that annoy me."

The woman sighed. Alex quickly grabbed the woman's hand and pulled her through the portal back to Wiz Tech.

Just then, they both dropped into the twelve-ball locker room! Justin was standing by his locker.

Justin looked at Alex strangely. "Who's she?" he asked in confusion.

"Hello," the woman said. "I'm the information-desk lady from Volcanoland."

Alex held her breath. She crossed her fingers that her plan would work. "Go ahead, Justin. Ask her a question."

"Could I get one of those uniforms?" he asked brightly. "I like the fringe things on the shoulders."

"No!" Alex cried. "A question about *Volcano-land*." But Justin was still admiring the uniform. Alex wanted to scream. They didn't have time for this! Dr. Evilini could appear at any moment. "Just tell him," she commanded the lady.

"At Volcanoland, more wizards have been drained of their powers than at all of the seventy-seven Wonders of the Wizard World combined. Wizards come from near and far to witness its awesome wizard-draining powers."

"Okay," Justin said, letting the information finally sink in. He looked at Alex. "So, you weren't messing with me about Volcanoland. But that doesn't mean Evilini's taking me there to drain my powers."

"Dr. Evilini?" repeated the woman. "Oh, she has a season pass to the draining section. And she paid extra, so there are no blackout dates."

Justin paced the hall. This was bad, he realized. Really bad—*and* dangerous. If he was drained of his powers, he could kiss being a wizard good-bye! "I've got to quit the tournament!" he exclaimed.

"While I'm here, would you like to buy an 'I Lava Volcanoland' T-shirt?" the woman asked.

"No, I don't want to buy an 'I Lava

Volcanoland' T-shirt, because I don't *lava* Volcanoland!" Justin exclaimed. Couldn't this lady see that he was trying to figure out how to defeat an evil wizard? He didn't have time to shop!

Justin grabbed Alex's hand, and they hurried off to find Dr. Evilini. There was no time to waste!

Chapter Ten

"**D**r. Evilini," Justin announced as he walked purposefully into her classroom. "Alex told me about your evil plan. I'm not playing in the twelve-ball final."

"Justin, Justin, Justin," the teacher cooed. She stood up from behind her desk and walked toward him. "I don't *have* an evil plan. Of course, Alex doesn't want you to have the twelve-ball championship belt. That would make you a shoo-in to be the one in your family to keep your wizard powers," she explained. She held up a thick silver belt. Justin stared at it. It was awesome. "There's a championship belt?" he asked.

"Mm-hmm." Dr. Evilini held it up so he could admire it.

Justin shook himself out of his daze. "Nice try, Evilini," he said. "I'm on to you. The Volcanoland information-desk lady told me.

The point is, I want to keep my powers. So I'm done. I quit. I'm out of here." Justin marched toward the door.

"You can't quit," Dr. Evilini pleaded. "I need to know who's the most powerful young wizard." She raised her arm and chanted, *"Scrittipolitti Noquitti!"* Then she zapped Justin with a bolt of electricity.

"Okay. I don't know what you just did to me," Justin told her. "But I still qui—I still qui—"

"You can't quit now. I put a 'no-quit' spell on you," she explained gleefully.

"I qui—I qui—" Justin couldn't get his mouth to form the words. "I want to play." Whoa! That was weird. "Oh, no. What am I saying? What am I doing?" It was as if there were two people inside him: the evil one who wanted to play and the good one who wanted to quit.

"Give me my Bidaddles!" Justin heard himself exclaim.

No, no, that wasn't right. "I don't want them," his good self said.

"I'm going to win," cried his evil self.

"No, you're not," replied his good self.

Justin wished his dad had taught him the counterspell to the "no-quit" spell. He knew without it, he had no choice. He was going to play in the big tournament.

Back at the Waverly Sub Station, the battle to see who could get more customers was still on.

"Try a salad right around the corner," called

the woman dressed in the salad costume. She passed out flyers to all the people walking by the Sub Station.

Max stepped forward and blocked her path. He was again dressed in his sandwich costume. "Hey, lettuce head!" he called. "Keep moving."

"I warned you about coming back here, shorty," she challenged. Then she heaved her weight into Max, knocking him off balance.

"Whoa!" Max exclaimed. She had shoved him hard—and he found it wasn't easy to defend himself when his hands were pinned inside a foam-sandwich costume! "I didn't want to do this, but you've given me no choice," Max told her. He turned and called, "Coo-coo."

The woman looked confused by his birdcall. Then a guy in a hot-dog costume appeared from behind a light post.

"Hey, Salad Bowl Girl! Remember me?" the hot-dog costume guy taunted. "Well, let me help you out. You thought you ran me out of business with that furniture arrow. But I'm not going anywhere."

The woman gaped at the guy in the costume. Then Max made another birdcall.

Suddenly, a woman dressed in a baked-potato costume, complete with decorations of sour cream and chives, and a man dressed as a soda can, strolled down the street.

"Oh, look. The rest of the combo meal is here," Salad Bowl Girl said, laughing at her own joke.

But no one else was laughing. Hot Dog Guy, Spud Woman, and Cola Boy stared menacingly at her.

"I can't believe it. I have always wanted to say this," Max said to himself. "I just never imagined it being this great." Max chuckled at the thought of what was about to happen. "Food fight!"

Just then, all the costumed characters

pounced on Salad Bowl Girl!

"Let me up!" Salad Bowl Girl cried. "You can't do this!"

"Had enough?" Max asked.

"Yes! I've had enough!" she shouted. She stood and brushed herself off. "My lettuce was on the ground," she wailed. "I'm a walking health-code violation."

"Thanks, guys." Max gave high-fives to his new buddies.

"We got her!" Hot Dog Guy cheered. "We got Salad Bowl Girl!"

Max nodded. He felt a little guilty about what they did, but for the family business, you sometimes had to fight dirty.

Max hurried inside his family's restaurant and changed out of his costume. The Sub Station was bustling with customers. He glanced at the clock on the wall. Max wondered if he could make any tips before his shift was over. His parents were taking him to Wiz

Tech to watch Justin in a sports tournament later that afternoon.

That school must have some awesome magic if my brother is in the finals! Max thought. Justin had never really been that good at sports. Max couldn't wait to see what would happen. But maybe his brother would have a great game plan like Max had had with Salad Bowl Girl. Anything is possible, thought Max. Even Justin winning a tournament.

Chapter Eleven

Alex excitedly entered the tournament room. A huge banner hung across the wall:

WELCOME
852nd ANNUAL WIZ TECH
Twelve-Ball TOURNAMENT

"Hey, you guys!" Alex called out to her parents and Max. She spotted them sitting on the stone bleachers that surrounded the twelve-ball table. "I have great news. Justin's going to quit the tournament."

"Why would he quit?" Mr. Russo asked. "That's not good news."

"I can explain," Alex began. "See—"

But before Alex could finish, Dr. Evilini pulled down a microphone from the ceiling at the center of the room and bellowed like an announcer at a boxing match, "*Wizards, student wizards, visiting parents, goblins, and ghouls—welcome to the Wiz Tech Twelve-Ball Finals. Our first competitor, well, what can I say? His name says it all. Jerko Phoenix!*"

Jerko ran into the room and everyone booed.

Dr. Evilini continued the introductions. "*And a newcomer to the sport and a serious threat, Justin Russo.*"

The crowd cheered as Justin jogged in. Justin smiled and waved to his family. "Hi, Mom."

Mrs. Russo smiled proudly. "Oh, look. He's waving at us."

The crowd let out another loud cheer, drowning out Justin as he said, "I don't want to be here."

But Mrs. Russo couldn't hear anything that Justin had just said. "I love you, too!" she called back.

Alex couldn't believe what she was seeing. This didn't make any sense. Why was Justin not quitting the tournament? "What's he doing here?" she asked aloud. "I told him not to play."

"You need to be more supportive of your brother," her mother scolded.

"I'm trying to save his powers from getting sucked down a volcano," Alex explained.

Alex's parents looked at each other and sighed. "We should really get her into a creative-writing class," her mom said to her dad. They both laughed.

This isn't funny, Alex wanted to yell. I'm not making up stories! But she didn't bother. It would take too long to explain everything. She ran over to Justin. "What are you doing?" she demanded.

"Dr. Evilini put a spell on me. I can't qui—" He fumbled helplessly for the word.

"First serve: Russo," announced Dr. Evilini over the microphone.

The crowd roared as a hand popped up out of the hole in the center of the twelve-ball table. Justin and Jerko took their positions on opposite sides of the table. The hand threw in the first ball. Then the second. Then the third. The game was on.

Alex slunk back to her seat. There was nothing she could do now but watch. Justin was under a spell, and there was nothing she could do to help him.

Gold balls were continually being thrown in, one after the other, as the two boys hit them back and forth with increasing speed and strength.

"He's got to lose," Alex said. "Lose, Justin, lose!"

"Alex!" her mother scolded loudly.

Jerko slammed a ball at warp speed toward Justin. But Justin reached under his leg with his Bidaddle and, in a move worthy of a circus acrobat, slapped the ball back at Jerko. The crowd went wild.

"I didn't mean to do that!" Justin called to Alex. He was playing on autopilot now.

"Way to go, son!" Mr. Russo yelled.

"Keep your eye on the ball!" Mrs. Russo advised.

"Miss it!" Alex screamed.

But Justin didn't miss. At all. His eye-hand coordination was off the charts. He hit back every ball Jerko tried to put away.

"Can someone please stop me?" Justin pleaded.

"Oh, my gosh, they're up to eleven balls!"

Hugh exclaimed. He sat next to Max. "No one's ever gotten to twelve before!"

The hand popped up from the middle of the table. It tossed another ball into play.

"The twelfth ball!" Hugh jumped up from his seat for a better view. "Get it, Justin!"

The twelve-balls whirred back and forth across the net. Jerko and Justin were focusing intently. As soon as they hit the balls, the balls zoomed right back at them.

Suddenly, Justin wound up. He swung. One, two, three, four, five, six, seven, eight, nine, ten, eleven—twelve-balls were blasted at once across the net! They hit Jerko's Bidaddle with incredible force, burning a large hole right through it. Jerko peered through the hole in amazement. He had lost.

"We have a winner!" Dr. Evilini announced. The crowd was on their feet. The cheers were deafening.

"I can't believe it! My brother's a champion!

Whoo!" Max performed a victory dance.

"Congratulations, Justin Russo. You are the best twelve-ball player in the entire school." Dr. Evilini handed Justin the shiny silver belt. His parents cheered enthusiastically. "What are you going to do now?" Dr. Evilini asked.

Justin balanced the belt in his hands. "I'm going to Volcanoland!" he announced. Then he gasped. Why did he say that? He didn't want to go there. Ever!

"You certainly are." Dr. Evilini let out her most wicked laugh.

"That's it. It's over," Alex said sadly. "I've tried everything." She couldn't believe it had turned out like this. "I just can't beat Evilini." She was defeated. "Justin's going to lose his powers."

"Who are you talking to, honey?" her dad asked.

"I am talking to myself," she admitted. I must really be upset, Alex thought. I'm acting crazy!

But just then, Alex remembered the spell that Headmaster Crumbs had used on her. Oh, what have I got to lose, she thought.

She faced Dr. Evilini and recited, *"Some are evil, some are kind. But now all must speak their mind."* Then she zapped her.

"So it's Justin," Dr. Evilini cackled. "I'll take him to the volcano and drain his powers for myself." She glanced around, confused. "Why am I saying this?" Then she realized. "Oh, no. A truth spell! They'll hear my plan to become the most powerful wizard!" She gasped. She'd said her secret out loud. "Stop talking!" she scolded herself.

Headmaster Crumbs, muffin in hand as always, stepped forward. "Security!" he called.

A guard in a light blue uniform grabbed Dr. Evilini's arm and led her away.

"I knew you could do it," Headmaster Crumbs told Alex. "You went to great lengths to help your brother and you brought Evilini down." He smiled at her. "When you apply yourself, you can achieve a lot more than you think."

Alex blushed. "I guess I can," she said shyly. She was proud that she had saved Justin.

"Hey, uh, when you were at Volcanoland, did you happen to buy a T-shirt in my size?" Professor Crumbs asked hopefully.

A T-shirt? Alex had been so caught up with saving Justin that she'd forgotten to shop. That was a first! "Uh, yeah, they're going to mail it to you," she fibbed. If she hurried there later, she could probably still get one sent. Everyone knew snail mail was really slow.

"Mm-hmm." He didn't look as if he believed her. *"Some are evil, some are kind—"*

Alex grabbed his arm before he could zap her. "Okay, maybe I didn't," she confessed. "But next time, okay?"

Headmaster Crumbs smiled. "Okay."

Alex smiled back. The headmaster was

pretty cool. Then she followed Justin over to their family.

"Oh, Justin. Honey, are you okay?" Mrs. Russo asked. She hugged her son.

"Yeah. Thanks to Alex," Justin said gratefully.

"I can't believe my baby almost had his powers drained in a volcano," Mrs. Russo said in amazement.

"We were very concerned," Mr. Russo agreed. His gaze landed on the silver belt Justin was still holding. "You still get to keep the championship belt though, right?"

Justin shrugged. He guessed he did. Somehow that didn't matter much anymore. He turned to his sister. "Alex, I'm kind of glad you came to summer school with me after all. Thanks for stopping Evilini from stealing my powers."

"So, from now on, you'll believe me?" she asked.

"You know what? I will. I think we've

grown up a lot this summer," he said honestly.

"Yeah, me, too," Alex told him. She placed her finger on Justin's sweater. "Oh, you have something on your shirt."

Justin refused to glance down. He gazed steadily at Alex. "I'm not falling for it this time."

Alex kept her finger pressed on his sweater.

I will not look down. I will not look down, Justin told himself. But what if she's telling the truth? He couldn't help himself. He had to look.

Just then, Alex flicked his chin with her finger and burst out laughing.

He'd fallen for it—again. He let out a sigh.

"Yeah, I saw that coming," Max commented.

Alex gazed around at all the kids in their black robes. Wiz Tech isn't too bad, she realized. In fact, I sort of like this school.

Alex gasped. I didn't just admit to *liking*

school, did I? she wondered.

Oh, but wait, it's *wizard school*, she told herself. A little magic always makes school more fun!

Something magical is on the way!
Look for the next book in Disney's
Wizards of Waverly Place series.

All Mixed Up

Adapted by Heather Alexander

Based on the series created by Todd J. Greenwald

Part One is based on the episode, "The Supernatural," Written by Matt Goldman

Part Two is based on the episode, "Alex's Spring Fling," Written by Matt Goldman

Justin Russo couldn't stop staring at her.

Her long silky blond hair shimmered in the afternoon sun. Her green-blue eyes were the color of the Caribbean Sea, and when she smiled, her face lit up the room. She was *beyond* gorgeous.

What he wouldn't do to have her notice him just once!

He would give away his entire collection of prized superhero figures to go out with her, he decided. But he knew that wasn't going to happen. *Ever.*

"Dude, close your mouth. Your tongue is going to dry out," his friend Henry joked.

Justin suddenly realized his mouth had dropped wide open. He took a swig of water from his water bottle. "You're right." He opened his textbook, trying to look as if he were doing something. Something *other* than staring at her.

"Listen, man." Henry nudged him. "Why don't you just ask her out?"

"*Kari Langsdorf?*" Justin gaped at his friend in disbelief. "I can't ask out Kari Langsdorf! She's got no idea who I am. She's never even talked to me. I'm totally invisible to her."

Justin turned his gaze again to Kari. She was standing by the front door of Tribeca Prep. A bunch of guys were gathered around her, and she was laughing. He leaned closer, hoping to overhear what they were talking about. Suddenly, his shoulder was shoved by a guy walking past him.

"Sorry, man." The guy grinned. "I didn't see you there."

"Why would you?" Justin muttered. It was the story of his life—*especially* his life in high school. "Totally invisible to everyone," Justin told Henry.

Justin watched the guy walk right up to Kari. No hesitation at all. Why would he hesitate? Justin reminded himself. The guy was a high school senior and looked like he belonged in the starring role in a teen movie on TV. He was the kind of guy girls like Kari noticed.

"Hey, Kari." The guy smiled, revealing straight white teeth. "You want to check out a movie this weekend?"

"Do you play baseball?" she asked.

The cute guy raised his eyebrows. "No. But

I'm quarterback of the football team, president of the student council, and I'm a swimsuit model."

"Oh." Kari seemed unimpressed. "I only date baseball players." She shrugged her shoulders and walked away from him.

Justin stared in surprise. If Kari wouldn't pay attention to that guy, he knew he should never think about even approaching her. Then he noticed that she was heading in his direction. She was coming his way!

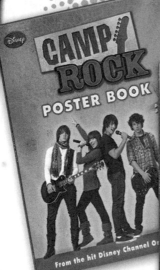

DS!